The Adventures of BUBBALOU

THE BABY WATER BUBBLE

By

Veenu Banga

To Mummy, who made all things possible.

For my children, who teach me every day, the meaning
of love, life, and forgiveness.

With gratitude to Samaniji Jin Pragya ji and Samaniji
Kshanti Pragya ji. Soul Doctors and Spirit Healers.
They shine a light to show the Path.

Remembering beloved Shailajaji. How did you know?
Your words have come to pass.

The catalyst for the publication of this book is my
Primary Care Physician Dr. Douglas MD. Best wishes to
Dr. Douglas for the next chapter of his professional
life. May he continue to raise the bar for Patient Care.

I am Bubbalou, the baby water bubble, I was born in the rain

With other bubbles and drips and drops I often float down a drain.

Sometimes into a field of flowers,
sometimes I fall on sod
I was born of the Lady Cloud, the
Thunder is her Lord.

Sometimes I flow into the gutter, sometimes into the sea

Where I join the mighty ocean, surfing along merrily!

I see many big ships pass, I watch racing dolphins at play

Sometimes I ride a big black whale like I am doing today!

The seas have turtles and octopus, bright corals on the seafloor

Seahorse, orange-yellow and spotted fish. Oh! The penguins I adore!

Then once again I pass through the air, into the clouds I go

This time I fall as rain into fields, where fruits and veggies grow.

Rain makes the farmers very happy,
on their orchards and farms we drop

Apples, peaches, carrots, greens, tomatoes, corn and rice, promise of a rich crop!

When next it rains, I come right back,
I fall into the trough below

Where horses, pigs and cattle drink up,
before on their way they go!

Cowboys take the horses for a run,
the cattle go out to graze

The pigs sit in their sties where they
take long naps and laze.

The chickens run into the barn so
their feathers can stay dry

But children have fun getting wet,
of rain they are not shy.

Once I fell into a pool, as boys and girls were swimming

Moms and Dads sat around cheering, the teams on to winning.

I daresay it was a lot of fun, and I raced in there with the boys —

After the fun and showers,
they headed home to books and toys!

Well, once again evaporated now, up and up and up, as air now I fly,

Meeting up with other bubbles to fill up the thirsty clouds in the sky.

Over roofs and hilltops in the clouds we float long and far,

Till it's time to rain down again, which Bobby collects in a jar.

He left the jar sitting on the window sill, one day, two days, then three

Off again into air the water goes, to join the clouds you see!

Cat knocks the jar down; Bobby
wonders where water goes,

Into the flowerbed below, of yellow sunflowers and red rose?

Once again gone in the air, the clouds hit trees near an enormous dam

I go through big pipes into the catchment areas, near Grandpa and Granny Nan.

The family is here to celebrate; it is Grandpa's birthday you see

Cake and candle, chips and dips, cookies, milk and iced tea!

When next it rains and you spot me,
and want to say Hello,
I'll do a pitter-patter dance for you,
before on my way I go.

And if you come out in the rain to join
me, and play in a puddle,
Take off your boots before going back
in, to stay out of trouble!